Books by Danielle Pafunda
Pretty Young Thing (2005)
My Zorba (2008)
Iatrogenic: Their Testimonies (2010)
Manhater (2012)
Natural History Rape Museum (2013)
The Dead Girls Speak in Unison (2017)
Beshrew (forthcoming)
Spite (forthcoming)

The Book of Scab

Danielle Pafunda

Ricochet Editions

Cover illustration by Bekah Fly
Book design by Betsy Medvedovsky

Published by Ricochet Editions
http://ricocheteditions.com

Ricochet titles are distributed by Small Press Distribution.
This title is also available for purchase directly from the publisher
www.spdbooks.org / 800-869-7553

Library of Congress Cataloging-in-Publication Data
The Book of Scab / Danielle Pafunda
Library of Congress Control Number 2018958759
Pafunda, Danielle

ISBN-13: 978-1-938900-26-6

FIRST EDITION

b e). e rn

Dear Mom and Dad,

I won't be home tonight. At the concert we ate a bag of soap powder that we bought for twenty-five ripped up sweaty dollars, and swallowed something a girl said was Tylenol and Eurydice.

There's a boy here who's been calling me Sister. He wants to know where True Love is, he wants me to follow him through the park, to leave some money in the base of a tree True Love often pisses on, to hold my hand and sit on the edge of the fountain until True Love comes back from the grave. He says that True Love is a beautiful man with twelve apostles who want us all to wash our feet before we come to the table he says that True Love takes his pants off and has babies all over the bathroom floor he says that True Love always knew I was a bitchcuntwhoreslut but he still wanted to feed me he says he says that True Love has a generous nature and will give us all plenty of time to please him before he sends us out to hustle for rent. He wishes I could've known True Love when he was alive he says True Love is coming back after the third set he says True Love comes on the wings of a guitar solo with a leather broom handle in his teeth riding a horse's skeleton.

I sit with that boy as long as I can and then, dying of boredom, tell him to wait for me there. That I'll be back, that I'll find True Love and come back for him. That of course I know what True Love looks like, he's only described True Love to me down to the tiniest detail of True Love's spent cock whimpering on True Love's generous thigh, wiry hairs on guard, True Love's favorite brand of cigarettes spilled out of the pack in a halo around True Love's bruised face, True Love's chest heaving, True Love's ingrown toenail throbbing in True Love's hoof propped on the arm of the sagging couch, its frame split, True Love's beer spilled, blending into the stained fabric, a pair of pliers dropped to the carpet a roach slipped out extinguishing itself in the dank shag, and True Love's colossal hand flung out in benediction.

I can see that boy from here. He's bent over holding a digital watch and counting on his fingers a contorted set of numbers. One of the speakers fell off the stage during the first act and crushed a girl's skull and one of the singers stuck his tongue on the microphone, which stopped his heart, but he was brought back to life by another band's singer and then they sang a classic rock love ballad duet, which they dedicated to not being dead. The band on stage now is performing shirtless in blood-soaked pants with knives at their throats they're playing their hit song about how much they hate each other's lovers, except for the drummer who's a four-hundred-year-old monk and never touches flesh.

It's getting darker. Our blanket is damp with smuggled vodka and piss. We know for a fact when they turn off the stadium lights you can fuck in the trees and sleep in the ravine. There's a party outside the north entrance, down deep in that crevice, so deep the lights from the parking lot wash over it like a visitation.

My boyfriend's best friend is there and waiting for us to show up so that he can pin me against one of the tree trunks and tell me again how much he loves me. He keeps telling me he can't live without me even though the sight of me shoving my tongue into my boyfriend's mouth makes him want to gouge out his eyes. He keeps telling me to take off my clothes more quietly, that he can hear me taking off my clothes and it's killing him. He tells me the elastic makes him die. The buttons rubbing on cotton are needles under his fingernails wishing for morning. He tells me when I squat to piss in the woods he hears heaven shouting his name. He thinks he could fit both my breasts in his mouth, he thinks he could suck the grief out of them. He thinks I rub my nipples before he comes into the room so that they're pointing at him, two tack-sharp accusers. He hands me a letter that he wrote on the crotch of my dirty underwear in permanent marker, and it says I need to shut the fuck up right now because every time I speak he hears me fucking someone else. He says I have the voice of someone who fucks every day, he says I have the face of someone you can't imagine fucking, he says I have the face of a dead girl from another century and someday I'll get a disease. In the letter, he says I'd better plug up my eyes because when I look at him he sees how possible it is for me to love him and he knows I'm just not trying. He wants to know what's wrong with me. He reads the whole letter aloud and then puts his mouth right next to my ear and says *tell me.*

Your Ugly Little,
Scab

Dear Mom and Dad,

In the culvert there are the bruised faces of elderberries and actual
bruised faces and I have slipped from a limb wet and greased and fallen,
hard along my left side. I have, you know, hit a man in the head with a
rock when he was still a boy and bent him over so sickeningly I myself
looked away. I have ridden a broken man up the sixty-foot banks, I
have looped my bad tail around him. At the top we found some hair and
condoms. We found some of your handwriting, or maybe it was the boys'.
We found her name scratched into the rocks if her name was indeed
you sweet bitch. Or maybe *you sweat bitch*. You bitch in the scuzzed out
campfire. You bitch seeing things projected over the fat, lank skin of
trees.

Oh. We bitches. Oh. We see certain things.

We trace over everything with a charred stick and in the morning and in
the morning and in what passes for morning on an overcast day too cold
to be actual summer, we see that all the tracings are of bodies and all the
bodies fashionably crammed into one another. My long scarf gets caught
in the mulberry tree. Mulberry, not elderberry. There's no such thing
as the past, here. There aren't any old-fashioned recipes, or any idylls
about the hymen. We piss into a little china cup with *England* carved in
the bottom. A little bluebell of a cup, tipped up, like so. I am tipped up,
cupped, concave in places where there used to be someone—someone
who used to be in this place.

What an empty pretty bag. What a pack of something what used to be in
there. And a bottle of. And an efficient blade.

You can't blame me for lying about the route we took. We took off
our shoes when it got very slick and scuttled into the future. Oh, here

we are. Oh, we are only one of us here, it's getting dark, in the wrong time zone, it snowed today before the sun went down. I talked to your proxies. I talked myself bluing the rain of flies on my forearms. And then nothing would do, so on I walked,

I'm just so ready to pop the screen and pour this mug of Goldschläger and Listerine out the window. I'm so ready to rip up this musty copy of *Tropic of Cancer*. I could put my boot through this speaker, through this album through the lead singer's leaded crystal skull through the drum's skull through the base drum through the skull of girls like me who get tangled up in their rooms listening to porn metal, taking the nettles out of their faces one by steely one until that face goes completely numb. Slack. And I'm ready to go facefirst out this window into the shimmy into the scuttle into the creek I'm ready to tell you what I found in your reeking leather suitcases.

Because, really, are you really so sure about my breath and bad makeup and the gash in my leg that never completely heals? When I'm spilling out all over the patio, even in company, and later when the company has gone and the petunias cling weeping and desperate, and even later when the defunct swimming pool fills with frogs, the tracks of raccoons leading back to their burrows, their dying faces petulant behind masks?

'Cause, gosh, these boys are WASPy. Gosh they're yummy and pale as their own behinds. I like to get my hands on them, my nails in them almost to break. I like to survey their torsos with my rigid tongue. Protestants, mostly, and one that makes skin flicks. Plastic, their wiry builds, their larger than average cocks, their bad taste in music. The old-fashioned men's books they steal from bookstores and hot-topic magazines they steal from work and list of guys who have/are bigger dicks than them and what they eat for breakfast nothing, for lunch a bag of corn chips and a cigarette, what they eat for dinner anything I have for them in a paper bag sheer with grease.

I'm moving forward with whatever regret-flavored filling I can jam in my pockets. Most of them know me by name. Most of them tumble out of my bed when your car pulls in the drive, or when Gramma comes over to chastise my face, or when they get phone calls from other girls who sell weed. Anyone who sells weed. Whatever.

Most of them know how to get here even though we live across town and down a dead-end street and there are dogs at one end and murder at the other and the mayor and the town beautification committee out on the wrecked triangle of public space the grassy delta that looks gray from misuse that's full of blisters and feral kittens, beer cans, economy.

I'm just so ready to flip up my dress to show you the cigarette burns and the colony of sparrows that's taken over my gut. I'm ready to show you this cheap gold leaf that's plastered to my throat.

Look close if you want, and I'll show you the scar on my face where the post went through where I rigged the front and back halves of a mule, where I rigged the head and the tail of a daisy, where I circled with kohl and I lined my lips with kohl and filled my teeth in kohl black and stitched through my cheek with medical grade gold thread and stitched through the webbing between thumb and forefinger my boyfriend's initials and then stitched over them when he left me standing outside the bakery with a bag of hash and a half-dozen crullers, I'm so stupid for sugar.

It's not that somebody loves me. Everyone loves me. Ever so briefly, then splits. And I, I never, I never ever ever have to hear them puke in the bushes again. You could take a note. You could take a hint. In the future, I'll be everyone's one night, and on that thousand-and-first, I'm going to burst. Feathers, rue, volcanic ash. I'll leave them a mess that can't none clean up, but—

Remember when I sat in my cradle, when I was a bab, when I sucked a baba, when I was just new to this world and didn't know the world had love in it or stars above it and didn't know the world had a smell other than ammonia and milk powder and didn't know there was a sidewalk you could skip down straight out of this world, this world? Remember when I was a bab and I didn't know any songs and no songs were sung and the whole world tilted toward dark and then back light again and no one ever mentioned it? When I sat in my cradle and counted all the letters in each of your names and added the numbers up until I came to the date of your death, but I didn't know what that was, I just knew it sparkled, a little jeweled fig from the future?

And then Great Gramma came to my cradle and gave me a lolly and told me how one day Great Grampa got so sick of the world and all the love in it and all the spring girl scents and all the sweet tobacco farm dinners and all the nickel soda movie jives and the music with its funny horns and the funny medicines you could buy from a man in the back room and the way a needle went oily in a flame's tongue and the way the same ray of sunshine swept in through the same rent in the curtain every morning across the same warped plank in the floor over the spot where he'd dropped his trousers but now they were hanging neat as you like 'em on the back of a chair even while the kids bawled in the living room until they learned that bawling wouldn't get them a sugar cube because when you're a bad little pony you'd best go down to the river and stay there 'til dusk, 'til he comes home hands stained with grease and skin breaking and hardly hungry it's another fish out of the river it's another fish passed by a corpse downstream, no one says anything, a corpse is just the cost of dinner, and so Great Grampa went out on the tracks where he put his head down on the tracks and the train came and crushed his skull?

And then she told me about the two pert girls in the convertible who were both decapitated by the tractor-trailer as they slid red and desperate and sideways beneath, in the past even though I couldn't comprehend how red convertibles existed in the past, perhaps she meant the present, I couldn't comprehend how she could know *anything* about the present because she was so fucking old?

And then she told me all her friends were dead and gave me a vanilla wafer in a cellophane package and called me by a more Irish name she preferred to my own and told me about all the famous murderers she knew in the city and how they would rub their tommy guns up against a girl and put a run in her army grade stocking and you could cheat them at cards but if they caught you it meant a knife in your ear or a hand up your dress and though they might send you a new dress in the morning your mother would never let you back in the house and, again, she paused, all her friends were dead. Then she showed me her pinkish scalp pulsing beneath that thin white net of hair? And then she was dead?

Before anyone else was born or old enough to know? When I was the only bab on the hearth. After the bells had rung, but before the ground thawed. After you started drinking, but before you stopped shattering that crystal bowl against the dining room wall, after I spilled on the carpet, but before you caught me wheezing in the crawlspace covered in fiberglass, after you paid the poison man, but before you came to in the driveway with the neighbors trying not to look as they scooted off to their day jobs, or after you tipped over the kitchen table and crushed one of the kittens that was always freezing to death in our yard, but before you hired the roofers next door to scrape up the kitten, and just before one of you shoved me up against the newly paneled wall while the other one of you lit a match?

There was a splinter working its way to my heart, a splinter works its way still. All the friends I ever had are gone.

Information crowds each pitiful cell, and this moaning thing that burrows under my ribs. My teeth ache a dull asynchronous ache, exiled from their skeletal kin. I'm like an elephant who's just become aware of the great distance between her heat and the tree. The great distance between the sob in her face and the bones of her herd. With my tusks, I'm moving something vulnerably soft across the grass. I'm lifting up the bones, those that used to be in our house, that used to be inside a person who lived in our house, who had thirty-two teeth and a lamp shaped like a tree, who had a sign on the wall that said I'm Okay, God Doesn't Make Junk, and a copy of The Trumpet of The Swan that I kept promising to read when I was old enough to make out all the words, but by then it was boring and I only wanted to read books about girls on the lam.

I'm using a scissor to cut through the thick skin on my feet, and to nip little vs in my forearms, I'm dabbing up all the blood with rose petals and silk like some sort of medieval courtly promise and eventually I'll cut off what's left of my hair and maybe also cut into my most somber dress and cut up the bedclothes and cut up this letter and stitch it back together so that what it actually says is Dear Mom and Dad, I'm a swan, all toothless and goo-hearted.

There's something soft in the bed with me. Something whose tissue folds weakly in on itself, something parted from its mother. There's something that might be wet, but it's too warm to tell. I think it's alive, in part, and writhing slow. I'm singing to it the low cuckoo song like a counterfeit lullaby. I got it off the radio from the future from the kind of music you pay too much for off a gritty blanket in the subway station because you're standing as far as you can get from the guy with the bruised and lolling cock and the two guys who look like they plan everything together and never sleep. It's a good enough song, it's putting us both to sleep with its no matter how high you build you keep missing your chance at the Lord, something old fashioned like that, slightly heretic a low bodice and a weeping lockback blade. A nightingale at the river plays fiddle, sobs out for his family, don't sob, clean-plucked sinner, huddled in the shelter of a dripping thatch, cold. In the glade go to seed, in the sun, dead lover, wink like a live one.

There's something I've been meaning to tell you. About that day in the water park when everyone drowned and the only child left in the pool was me, and I'd a bloody feather tucked in my crown? I didn't mean to do it. I meant to do it well.

This, a tether between syrup and sort behaving oddly. It runs hot, pounding up into the pink gloom, an orphaned seal pup, mired in slurry, over again.

It runs high as an engine now, takes names, slurs them in mud. It grips by the hair, throat, wrist. It wrenches cartilage and spits in a way that can be framed as assault, but when the police come they have a piece of paper and a pair of tongs and a wink instead of a warning.

We get a letter from the hospital asking for another week in my spine. We assent, we bring them me and they go into my gates with the crude keys. We ask them to make a graph of these cryptic fluids and strangely isolated citizens. The lymphocytes are fat with longing. Nothing in me scans pure enough to count as itself. One after another, my cells rise to the surface and burst. Oh, love! Oh, any other body in whom I could bury my hot, raw eyes. Stupidly strung to the window's split frame, hatched as a tin can, all manner of laceration coming my way.

Then it was spring. I hitched the screen, a shower of flies their bodies making discreet patter, a skin sound, a wet patch of kin, all piled up in the least dank corner. I'm capable of that least little kindness, you know. It's the very least. The lease signed, the least done.

Watching the kitten hemorrhage in her cardboard box, as you instructed, as you left us there. I could loop the reel repeatedly 'round its neck, but actually I can't. I'm every type impacted. This continuation wolfpact, this tacit agreement that it's live or live endlessly, and so I let spacetime's meshes pronounce every syllable in my stead. It's film. It slits my gills as I surface.

I'll say this once: I'm an only child. No matter how many siblings you cook up in there, no one else will ever cite you. No one else will play your mumblety-peg. It's always you and me alone in this gray metal drawer, bare bulb fetal, scissoring above us. I will go decades without input from the sibyls. I will gird my house with salt. When the time comes that it is no longer feasible to love you, I'll walk willingly into that severed state that is either real or Freud's hoodwink or whatevs, Mom and Dad.

So long, lazy Scab, eating your food and breathing your air and your share of the fiberglass, your share of the romantic disease, your share of the sugar spilled deep in the rug, grain moths, raw spices, everything you need to make a bomb. For what feels like the millionth time, my vision compresses, my harp twitches, my mouth numb around nouns, until I flail into it, hardly unwilling, hardly wanting to stop.

So instead I will work for food, for fuck's sake, for work-for-it. I work for Dad. I spend a lot of time in the pit. I strap on these boots every morning so my feet won't rot in the pit, but begin to rot in the boots.

It's nothing to me. In the photographs the children have plastered their faces with a mix of rust and gristle they call futureblood and I know which ones will soon all too soon lie down on the tracks.

To wrap the merciful cord of an old rotary phone around our necks in an abandoned rental on the back of a property that belongs to a filmmaker from the city, to lie still while spiders crawl in and out of our hair, to lie still while they rearrange our feet, to lie still draped with a transparent shower curtain across a midsection below the nipples, a thigh hanging out, the era of long hair flowing over shoulders, but so still like baby seals clubbed pink.

I become the one in charge of the grosgrain ribbons, I load up my bag with magazines, I hold people's shivering babies, I sell a box of skin at five a.m., at midnight, in broad daylight. It's anything, all work, the furthest point on the fattest train.

When they find my body petaled in plastic, when my lips blue as blue roses in an icebox smooch, call the beautiful detective. Call my best friend in her pleated skirts and my boyfriend the baller. Call loud—

When they find my ant-laced ear in the field, stay out of the grid. The roar of heaven in my wind-swept ear, my ear partial to the ground, my ear that heard every last but can't tell you a single thing. Stay back. Cast your noir shadow on the stairs as you climb, or shiver your pistol a toy of a thing uncanny in its potential. Make a work of sipping your coffee, make a work of straightening your hem.

When I'm playing a decade under my age.

When I'm as close as a prophet to the bare behind of my protector, when he's knocked backward, when he's tumbling over me I'm an ill-placed dog, when he's dead at my feet, when the seam collapses on us—

It's fully funded, all cherry-bombed out, ground up hide-n-seek, oh! I'm wrung with spandex and wrung out, oh! leaking drawstrings, leaking bubblebleach, smelling sweet as Easter. I'm nothing but an old old soul, digging out your rotproof jumpsuit, your turtlenecks with the wicked implications and the sluggish aim. I'm basement crouching in the cedar closet very surely mapping out the future with a sticky pair of pinking shears, a dead kitten lodged right up there in the drop ceiling, crooning, a kitten dying from a fall, a kitten in the oil burner with his stupid kitten daydreams, or a hole behind the furnace where all the kittens go.

I'm woozy from it and running out of nails to dig, a plain patch of skin where I can draw a heart and carve in it how much I *love you.* I can carve in it *who brought you here.* I'm sixteen screaming horses drug and dragged and awfully sentimental.

There's a fake panel in the back of the closet, and I can pry it open with a wire hanger. If I disregard my bleeding hands. There's a thousand thousand dollars in there. A diamondback pistol. A can of paint. More things. There's a passport, but it isn't your passport and it hasn't got your picture in it. A naked, fuckfaced passport. There's a photo album swollen shut, the color rips out when I pry open a page, the handwriting bleeds, there's a box of nails, bolts all different sizes. This isn't my hideyhole, but even so my face grows hot.

Oh. Don't I have feelings. Oh, don't I get a little bell-like shudder, a sound rung out from under my lampshade. Don't let me leave the house looking like this in the shroud of your greasy young ambitions.

Don't I want to be cool as cool as waterfall as catwalk as stars swaggering out of my bed. They fail into their t-shirts. Or the girl whose wing is on fire in her bedroom, some white panic melancholy playing, old kind of stereo bourge-fuck, shorting out when the vase of dead roses tips over on cue, frosting the room with its vegetal weeping, where did they even, because no one lives like that.

And don't anyone look ungrateful, because you'd otherwise have died in there.

You'd otherwife have never married like you do so often in the future, on the lawn, never have made it look so checkered bright with normal no matter how you had to rig it up.

And don't look. Don't look what I'm dragging up out of the basement when I come with my skin weeping and the rings under my eyes like the poem about the pale Russian corpse, when I come up after three days, air thick and oily, the only songs the kitten songs. When I come up leaking a heap of slips, when I burn through it, when I burn a series of holes down the front of the wedding gown and thread a red nylon scarf through them, when I lash a pair of trousers around my waist and seal them at the ankles with duct tape and in the loose legs carry the bodies of kittens. The can of paint has burst in the heat and splattered me, and the whole tableau gets wasted in the front yard.

Here's a long scrap of rough lace I wind 'round my forehead. Scrub my mouth and stand in the road with those horses bearing down, my name imprinted backward on my cheek, my name shuddering off-track, snagging not a single wire in the search, nowhere on even a loose sheet, bottom of the mildewed box, not in anyone's glove, anyone's plagiarized hamburger-meat version of the past. I'm still devoted to all that rust.

That pinching sensation you both experience in the night is pinching, me pinching you. Good thing you snore so hard, good thing you eat everything in sight and then drink all the Tom Collinses and then howl until you knock your heads on the headboard and pass out bleeding just a little from the temple.

I have the same nightmare every night. It's called *How to Get Out of the Yard*. It's called *Fuck You to Death in the Yard*. It's called *Hanging From the Rafters Drying Out Like a Carcass*. It's called *The Fence is Down*. It's called *Digging Out*. I have the same nightmare every night and then I wake up standing in the hall outside your door.

In I come with my pinchers. My pincers, my pinkers, my nails as fine as fiberglass, my fingers cold as winter root. Right up under your covers with a pinch. Because what did you tell me about it? *Pinching causes cancer. Every pinch is an act of war, every pinch incites cellular division, if you want to cause cancer keep doing that, right there, do you want to give us all cancer?* With my filthy fingernails. With my fingers sore from all that hard work pinching. All the damage underwater, all the damage a lie I could tell that I didn't do it, credit I never receive for being the kind of patient girl genius who doesn't mind waiting on a disease that won't take effect for another forty years.

With my urgent fingers, I come creeping. To keep it up, to divide, to create anew, to fashion someone out of you. To fashion two newer bodies, to replace you with dough, to replace you with legions, to fill up the bed, to smother, to account for the kittens you've killed, to account for the punch lines. Or else like a horticulturist. A bud I nip, a graft or splice, an anatomist measuring twice.

Otherwise, I pinch myself, I pinch the covers tight between, I pinch a tissue full of fur, I pinch the fox stole and its satin innards, I pinch sugar,

I pinch the fat layer over my hips and the fatter layer over my thighs, I pinch it to death and it blooms.

I pinch everyone and everything, but never money, I don't know why. I should rip you off more often. I should be ripping you off this whole time. The stupid wads in your pockets, the money you drop in the sink, the stacks of bills the bars of silver the jewels you sock away under the beds, the jewels you have set and reset and wear out to the grocery and wear to the morgue when you go visiting and wear to the cemetery to pick out your own plots the best in the business and wear to dinner and dinner and dinner and wear when your poor relations come calling and wear when you carve up the meat for dinner and wear when you wash up and in the tines are tiny threads from the meat, the jewelry you tell me I'll have to stand very very very still to catch and I can have it when you're dead.

The money you pour into the back of strangers' trunks, the money you turn into guns and knives and lengths of rope. You buy a property, you buy a boat, you put a bigger stronger faster engine in every bitch's chest. You're so rich, Mom and Dad. You have a million dollars. You have six hundred pewter figurines spelling out your name on a heavy crystal platter, you have a classic car with white leather interior made from rabbit skin and a Camaro. You bought a dead bird re-stitched and strung, wired into a music box with an act of flight so real we duck every time it opens.

Your Ugly Little,
Scab

Dear Mom and Dad,

Here I am sweeping up from the latest suicide party, spilled pills, jack-knifed shotguns, photos smashed from their frames. At your wedding the priest bit the rabbi and the rabbi was sore, and everyone rabid on that foaming bowl of punch. Then I was born, bruised and fat from the squalid pigeonhole Mom calls a body, and she turned me in to the cops, three days old, for homicide attempts.

Here you are now, trying to take it all back.

No wonder I'm so tragically boring, no wonder I'm such a non-stop whiner. I say everything twice, I have only myself for reference.

Only. I eat the entire baggie of mushrooms and when my soon-to-be-dead friend ditches me for a better party I hop on the back of the nearest urgent animal. I hop on his alien back, his otherworldly horse back, his loping back copper-stunk and studded with bones. I ride him smoothly into a glade and read an article about the occult practices of high-stakes day traders while someone goes down on me. In the glade, it's like every movie I've ever seen lush, like a stupid planet full of languageless bear children about to be obliterated by an even lusher, sadder orb. I have a stable feeling. I have the feeling that everything I do is sound and that I'll be a-okay and then the feeling starts to fade and I can't do anything about it. Do you know how stark that is? I can't do a thing to feel. Then my body trundles along, oh little Scab, hobble off and take a pee—

This isn't really me. This is the suicide I've always dreamed of. This is the *kill kill* I get to cram in the creek's bloody molar. This is the fuckstop this is the piece of muscle scavenged from the wreckscape. In the hand the handle sits heavy and meaningful, with the knowledge of where one rib is sewn to another, with the knowhow of an upward thrust, with the complete conviction that this gesture can end it. This is not me, but the image-tic that wakes me, the ickickickickickick that stutters through a tightly woven fabric of protists, bacteria, potential.

In the future, when she/it/me walks along the ridge of the mountain that whores out its fossils and frowns on us grievously, she'll never admit to having known this/it/me. In the future, even bearing my own broken fingers, even marking the earth with the same carbon burn, she will say, *Who, now?*

This is ahistorical. This is perverse presentism. This is the normate fucking her way into a dilettante's pose.

I don't want to know you, do I?

This is the longing I had with my head gone squeamish between the speakers and a mouthful of shag rug. Where I ruined my skin with crying, this is where I ruined my skin with scalding, this is where I drank a bottle of witch hazel and promptly puked it back up. This is where I ate raw nutmeg and saw the future. In the future I was a talking wolf and I told the boys to get a head start. I ran through town, capeless, full of pearls, shedding. In the park, I climbed the gazebo and on its pitching roof I pitched.

I'm doing the best I can to be—

Your Ugly Little,
Scab

Dear Mom and Dad,

I don't ever plan on saying anything right. I don't plan on ever getting through the whole day in public dry and in good hands.

The day when I leap from the rafters of the boathouse in the park onto the back of that really beautiful boy, the one who looks like a deer when he moves, who rows and all his muscles threaten to leap up from his body and turn into doves and sing their way to heaven, that boy, who isn't very smart is he, but who cares, he's got the smartest mouth he's got the rightest cock.

Not that I've seen it, yet. I leap in wet from the lake and nuzzle, all my skin roughing against him. I leap and crown him with my wet fists and give him a sovereign licking, and even then—did he? He lit on his hooves and ran.

I devise a way to get into his house by making friends with his mother. I make my new boyfriend break into his house and fuck me on his sheets. I spend the night outside his house watching the pattern of lights go off and then the lights come on again just after dawn. I give his father the keys to your cars I give his father a bottle of your black label Jack Daniels I give his father some of the pornos I found in the ravine just in case he likes that kind of thing. I give his father my lowest look up through lashes, just in case. Whatever.

If he had a sister we'd be best friends, and I'd be over every night, light as a feather stiff as a board, I'd be over every night curling each fine strand of her hair and securing it with a wire pin and painting the name of her lover in fragrant butterfly letters across each of her perfectly arced nail beds. I'd be holding his sister when she heard a noise from the yard, and tailing after her when the noise became her lover and he'd brought his friend and we slipped out the window into the dark, two agile deergirls disappearing into the mouth of a flask.

But instead his mother collects ceramic dolls and I help her to name them. She lines the dolls up on a bed of their very own, full-sized, with a canopy, she has the canopy embroidered with children, or dolls, playing games of jacks, picking the petals off daisies. She keeps the names of the dolls on stiff cards that she props in their hands, she records their dates of birth in an enamel diary with a crystal pen.

She collects instructions from the dead, she tells me they said to stop cooking pork, to watch out for letters from strangers, to wear her right earring but not her left, to lie when asked for her mother's name, to lie about her own date of birth, to lie about her son's name and date of birth, to lie to the bank, to apply for a loan, to fill the pantry with cans of pineapple and pumpkin meat, to burn her husband's sports magazines, to burn his ties, to bury his tie clips and business cards in the backyard, to bury his Bob Dylan albums, to break his John Lennon albums into small pieces and wait for the ghost of Yoko Ono to arrive, to burn the tax returns, to burn the curtains in the dining room, to drink a gallon of tomato juice every day, to pluck out her eyebrows, to pluck back her hairline, to outline her hairline with a black pen, to clip her eyelashes short, to thread a needle with fishing line and tuck it through the fabric of her bra, to carry razor blades in a candy tin in her purse, to stay in the house all of August, so I have to get her out before then.

I send her a flyer for a doll show that happened six years ago so I black out the date and photocopy it with tomorrow's date scrawled in and when tomorrow comes I go to the house and she's pulling out of the driveway and on the front steps a life-sized ceramic golden retriever looks longingly for her return. I skirt the porch, hop the fence, and squat down in the backyard, but I don't really need to because the boy who looks like a deer is there all by himself now that his father never comes home, in the kitchen with the curtains drawn back with all the lights blazing, making dreamy eyes at absolutely nothing, eating raw vegetables and playing records that turn me off, but he's so beautiful it doesn't matter.

Then I'm in the kitchen breathing heavy and he recognizes me from school, from the lake, from the time he put his finger in my cunt and told me a story about Neil Young. I've got that record on in my suitcase record player, in the itchy back of my mind, in the hot place in my belly, it's playing *rust never sleeps* or *cinnamon girl* or some awful sound that I'll never be able to stomach again. Or it's simply his record playing in the kitchen and it's playing extra slow just to prove to me that no one else knows it's go-time.

I tell him *it's go-time*. I tell him we don't have to spend any money and I tell him about my boyfriend's other boyfriends so he knows it's no big deal, and I tell him about how I have this really sore spot on the small of my back, right where a tail would be. I give him my hands so he can see how fucked up my lifeline is and then I offer to cook him something. I take eggs and cheese out of the refrigerator, but I can't find the frying pans and I start crying a little, and he tells me his mother buried them in the backyard. Instead, I fill a tall glass with ice cubes and pour in the Jack Daniels and add some Coke and stir it with my finger and hand it to him, and he sniffs it but doesn't drink it because he's in training, his beautiful muscles are each training to go to heaven, a thousand glittering doves. I didn't mean to say that aloud, but it seems like I have so I tell him again that my boyfriend doesn't care and I take off my shirt I'm standing there in just my bra. He's sitting down where I can press my torso against his, and then he stands up so tall, giving me a faceful of his fluttering stomach.

But then one of those dead ladies comes down from the attic and tells him he's smarter than anyone gives him credit for and looks at me cross-eyed and suddenly I'm the Styrofoam from a rotten package of chicken thighs, and there I go out the back way into the alley, where I'll stop, I mean really I'll stop for him, like he'll never again– Like the way naming me as you did, giving me this rhyming absence of a call sign makes sure no one ever gets their hands all the way 'round my neck. Oh, right, so thank you. Thank you, I'm much, much better off.

What has become of these exquisite boys? They have their arms slung round each other's necks and are singing something from the worm radio. They're each over six feet tall. I feed one of them a bruised apple from the bottom of my bag and he claims it gives him an erotic convulsion. Another one rubs his hands up my thigh and begs me to be more A-list. There's a third one, swaddled. A fourth one with his spine sewn down. More. They're drinking beer with red food dye in it, and when they vomit, slick little disks of dye will spill out across the tile floor. They're eating every sack in the pantry and playing a video game about true love. They sleep on couches in each other's bedrooms and give each other a yum just to see and become morose when it's nothing new or wonderful.

They pay me five dollars to lick a girlfriend's face, and five dollars more to steamroll her. One of them pays me five dollars to stop. We hike through the deadghostcorpsetown woods to the convenience store where I buy a candy bar and a wind-up plastic mouth from a vending machine. Like the mouth, I'm a mouth on legs, and like the mouth I'm chattering. I bandage my face, I wrap my shirt around my face, I dump out one of the boys' backpacks on the linoleum floor and jam my head deep inside, and the clerk asks to see proof. I'm concave, just as you made me, all the skin and none of the substance. Between my ribs there are failings, and in my lungs there is a swollen crown of pollen spurs. It's the only thing natural about me. I cough, and my bad taste wheezes out.

I cough and suddenly there's a tongue in my mouth not my own, a legion of tongues, a rotation of sour tongues. I mean, it's Saturday, it's the summer, everything ripe's fallen off trees and rotted already, all the dogs are drunk, all the boys blow smoke at the dogs, the kittens are damaged from falls, the vinyl tearing off the car seats stuck to thighs in the uncompromising heat, the radio shorting out and strung

together with aluminum foil weeping all over itself, I'm on the roof of
the car now, swallowing, waiting for the show to start, plucking gravel
out of my knees—

All these waxless wax dolls thick with winter spunk, bracing themselves, their knees in each other's backs, against the seat backs, their earbuds jammed deep, their hoods pulled close against bangs against foreheads, those foreheads pressed to the windows perilously close to cauterized phlegm or jizz or scratched out slurs, the kings who died here before us.

I imagine the bus driver's bald pate shining up from between my thighs, a flake of sebaceous skin drifting away on a draft. The school bus driver. His spectacles, his oily grin. I imagine him pinning my wrists and dragging my jeans down to my ankles, how cold the seat will be on the small of my back, his knees getting filthy from the melted slush everyone tracks up the aisle.

In the background, the radio is Top 40 self-loathing, plunging forward off each bridge, compulsive. With his tongue pointed, turgid against my thigh and then my cunt and then pausing to yell out what a rank little pup, returning to the job, my hips rolling up so that I'm visible to anyone whose glance slicks over, waiting for us to pull back on the highway, finish the job.

I dream the whole way, the dolls, their heavy brows knit, thinner than thin bodies, wicking tears.

We crash the bus and live in the hollow by the park. We go into a partially excavated cave and each of us must for the good of the community get pregnant by one of the boys, or the bus driver, or all of us by the bus driver, or by the one boy who wears our scarves strung together in a long leash like a prize as we lead him from pallet to pallet, who cries out for his mother when he's sore and empty, and we pet him, but we're no solace for anyone, now.

Where we eat, drink, and wash our faces in snow. Where we are beautiful with freezing cold, the blood sucked into our middles, a thick pool of it, our limbs in various shades of porcelain and ash. Where on holidays all the town's unwanted children get dumped in our park, with flashlights and new sneakers, and whichever ones are clever enough to find their way back to the road will be picked up on buses and returned to their parents. From the ditch we pick favorites and cheer them on.

We build traps for the piggy ones, traps for the whiners and the ones who smell like puke. We keep those losers and let them sleep at the foot of our burrow in a pig pile until they're old enough to drink.

In this dream, though, we never actually give birth. We stay full forever. We don't love each other or any of the boys, and we don't love our pets. We move smoothly without feelings from past to present, we govern by nods and tilts of the head, we sleep in a heap of velvet robes beneath a snow bank no human can dig through, we never go home again, we never use our old names, we never write back, we lie back, we lie in the snow on sunny mornings our blood bleached, our stomachs round and high, drifts themselves, ice babies rolling smoothly beneath, we don't want anything, you can't have us. We never actually wake up wet and screaming, starving to death, as I am sure to do in this green plastic seat, any minute now—

When they ship us out into the fields, someone immediately steps on a nest of sweat bees, and we all get stung. They send a retired nurse out to see if anyone's dying and she smells like gin and menstrual blood. The nurse has her own bone saw and a pair of latex gloves she washes and dries on a loop of twine hanging from her belt. The nurse finds three of us swollen and wheezing, ready for her hospital beds. The rest of us stay in the field, inching forward carefully.

My bee won't die. It suctions to my ear, a gray jewel pulsing. It tells me things about life underground, about life in a hive, about living dead. It tells me that it spent its entire life looking for me and now I'm the one who gets to kill it. It tells me that the winters have gotten colder and the springs are wetter and drier and earlier and that tornadoes and blizzards and beetles are coming nearer, that the radiant devices make it hard to breed, that its own mother died in a vat of paint and its hive can only find pollen in a few of the flowers. It tells me that everything we've ever heard about chemicals is entirely true. It tells me that I was born dead, too, it tells me that we have unidentified substances in our blood, it tells me that unlike a bee, I'll die with my weapons intact, I'll die with a neat set of knives and semi-automatic weapons stacked beside me, I'll die with a can of mace and a noose packed tightly in a bag, I'll die with someone interrupting me, I'll die with my face poised to open and speak, I'll die with six varieties of meat in my freezer and no one to catch me.

My bee has been waiting forever for me and it won't stop squirming. It digs deeper into my ear, it tells me that we've only just begun, that we are a superior being locked in its deathy embrace, that I'm purified by my nearness to the bee, that it could smell me sweating a mile away, that my sweat told it to come to me, that my sweat is my only saving grace, is the only thing about me that isn't putrid with lies, that as long as the bee pulses into my ear I am a glory, that it has a thousand brothers and sisters but I am the only one it really loves, me—

Your Ugly Little,
Scab

Psssst,

I'm doing something I can't talk about. I'm unbearable organ by organ, in quarantine for the glum. In the papers there's mention of an underground sugar society. Syrup in the governor's chambers. I get out my scrapbook and paste the articles to its urine-stained pages. I think I'll want to remember this. I think, in the future, I'll pretend I was a part of something. In the walk-in freezer that stands in for the heart of this town, we put all the deer that've yet to be butchered. We collect the deer in chest drops at two gas stations and the library. We take their velvety muzzles in our palms and whisper their human names to them as they cross over, disoriented, still rooting out the tulip bulbs. When we get turkeys, we hardly bother. When we get a rabbit, we separate the boot from its lining in one swift gasp. I don't have any blood on my hands, but I have plenty in my throat. Tomorrow, when I open the freezer, its eye will leap out at me. Its marble black eye, still swimming with questions. A long blade of grass stuck in its hoof.

When the catastrophe comes, I'll feel proprietary, entitled to its honeyed passage. Until then, I go around so lonesome I could die. Until then, I have my ex-boyfriend's tooth mounted on a post and I wear it hilariously through my pierced lip. You want me to be better than this, no mascara or candy necklaces, but I'm addicted to plastic and off-gassing. I'm addicted to cupcake wrappers, coated in a thin layer of crumbs, sticky-rimmed, I suck them into dissolution. When nobody's home, I hunch over on the couch picking my nose. Then I do this on the bus, and no one notices. I go into a toilet stall and leave a letter to the editor in its tampon box. There's a world under this world where our dead selves hang waiting for our bodies to get it over with. There's a world just for the embarrassing things we shamed ourselves saying when we were cheerful and careless.

Hey! I have a sard-red tatter with a precious letter stitched on it! The letter A! The letter F! What? You're dead and I'm alone on a brand new continent. You're dead but you come back to life as my *husband*. He's missing. He's at sea, or he's banging natives until he infects them all with his Dutch hazards. When I get out of prison I go live at the edge of town, because I know how much it costs to live in town. The ravine is full of rusted husks, VINs redacted, distended drive shafts, nude and reeling. The ravine is full of diggers. The roads are full of men looking to make hay. Hey fellas, with your 150 thousand gallons of chemicals: can you find me the road from here? Oil's running down my legs. My little girl pegs you in the head with a rock or hunk of cinder. *You can't run your car on sunshine, sunshine*, she sings, and I wish to hell I were my little girl instead of me, but this is just a story. This style is dead! Pin it to my chest, this dead letter office. A confession! Oh wow! Keep it in the customs house.

Dear Mom and Dad,

We're all in a play and the director keeps feeling up the other girls backstage. All the white girls. He doesn't cast the black girls or the Asian girls. He casts a Latina girl, but she's six feet tall and punches him in the mouth and quits the show when he asks how her tits got so big so fast. He doesn't cast the Indian girls, but he asks a Persian girl to do the lights. He doesn't touch me. He doesn't seat me so that my dress hikes up, or ask me to cross the stage in a slip without a bra, he doesn't care if I wear glasses or not, and never replaces my iced tea with Wild Turkey. He brings me a list of props that I'll need and all the props are appropriate to the show, even though I saw him earlier gesturing at a pink-blond white girl with a bright pink dildo and a pair of pliers. Up in the costume loft, in a dusting of dead flies, he pushes another white girl back on her heels and nuzzles her stomach. He leaves an extra-wet trail of saliva across the front of her sheer robe and tears some of the feathers from her carefully crafted hair. The Persian girl who does the lights carries her back down to the edge of the stage and hands her a cigarette and a Twizzler and asks if she's on the pill.

The director licks the pancake from the chest of the biggest white girl, he takes one of the boys out to buy more lumber, he writes a new scene into the script that requires quick changes backstage and asks the black girl stage manager to make sure that no one's wearing panties. He changes his mind about the Asian girls and sets up a bubble-filled tin tub on stage and tells the two Korean girls who sit in it and sing a song from *The Pajama Game* that no one will guess that they're actually naked. When I walk over to his desk, he hands me a broom and asks me to sweep up all the false lashes. He asks me if I've found the right shade of red for the star's big luscious fat suckface mouth. He asks me if I think he made a mistake about the Asian girls, if I know where to get Ecstasy, if I have the phone number of the Latina girl who quit the show. His ruddy head blends into his ruddy face blending into his flesh neck where his collar perches and his v-neck sweater calls up ruddy welts, tucked into his pants, neatly pleated across his lap.

He has a wife. He shows me a picture of her and asks me to buy something in her size at the grocery across the street. I buy a pair of pink latex gloves and a plasticized apron printed with teapots. He asks me to try on the apron and when I cinch it tight across my bare back he just says it will do. The black girl who builds the sets makes a *tssk* and one of the white girls from the garden party scene laughs behind her hand.

When the director calls the rest of the cast in for notes and tells the lead to tape her tits together everyone argues about the best kind of tape. He tells the white girls in the chorus to keep their legs high, and tells the boy playing Stanley to get one of the Indian girls to oil his chest. He tells me to wash my face, he tells the Indian girl who sews costumes to sew him a smoking jacket for the cast party, he tells the boys to bring all their rope and all their trading cards, he tells the prettiest white girl to pick one of the boys from the chorus and show him how it's done, he tells the prettiest black girl on the crew to go along and take notes, he tells me again to wash my face, he asks for his glasses he makes a note in a little notebook with a nude by Degas on the cover he asks for his flask back from the lead boy he asks for a couple goddamncuntandwhore aspirin, he cries a little and tells us we can't imagine how long he's waited for this, how long he's been teaching US history in the shitforbrainspodunklittle school, how long he's hung his dong out the window on dark nights just waiting for the muse to come and suck the wonderpoison out, how long he's been making do with the hole he drilled into the girls' bathroom through which he threads a tiny fiber optic microphone that broadcasts back to him the sound of piss on porcelain, how long he's had his hat in the ring, how many times he's struck and struck out and been under the strain of it all.

I'm speaking to you sweet as cream punch because what are you going to do when a girl like me turns to you with her lips in a bow, sweet as cream punch, creamed? I'm speaking kindly, my lips hardly move when I speak, I'm a frosted cherry, cherry malt, I'm a straw punched through a maraschino, I'm neon red, red-and-white striped, I'm beachy sweet, a sugar dolphin with my eyes lit up. In one clenched fist a melting nonpareil, in the other a safety pin.

I've got every costume rigged to go, I've got my feet in the stirrups and my arms through the suspenders, I've got an architecture of boning tugged down over my jelly. I've got ringlets. I've got bells that announce my coming and a thump that says I've gone. Let me pretty for you out here in front of all these lookyloos. Let me pour it on thick, with my extra dusting of I didn't mean to, but then my turn isn't coming up, my hand is slackening, my crook goes sailing as I wave down in a swoon, into the orchestra pit, ruining the band's clean reputation. I'm salt in all their instruments, I'm the unfortunate incident in their first lapse of judgment, interrupting the show.

Why I wrote all those horrible threats on sheets of flypaper and wrapped them around the cellist's bow. Why I couldn't stop slapping at the girls in French horns and penny loafers, or how I got it into my head to stuff the snare drum full of kitten fur, or why I put a gallon of Borax in the tuba. Why I'm always in the hatchback of some loser's car, with a list of phone numbers scrawled up my arm trying to give directions home.

Around three AM this sweet little deadeyed bunny shows up at the party with a trash bag full of strawberry frosteds. I've been in and out of this dress. I've been stretching my corneas like they open up into another world called *me* and I tell everyone what a really great place that is, and tell them *now get inside, motherfuckers*. I'll get a knife out of the kitchen and claim I can see the future in it. And brush my teeth until it feels good. I ruin everything, don't I, when I go looking for affection, when I go looking for it—

Indicate to me that it's acceptable to feel this way forever. In my ribcage, which is broad and shallow, I've got perpetual conviction. A gilled sliver of phosphate on the bone shadow frog-kicking back up from under river, taking the steps by two, leaping shank-limbed so cheerful into bed! Precious flesh kin! My chest withers and blooms with it, a new organ feinting over the old one. But as it turns out, I won't go. I won't into night either rage or whimper. Instead I follow a cranked-up voice into the basement of a half-built display home. I'm a saunter-free drownedfaced pilgrim. My head a searchlight, my heart a slippery eel brocade all turned out for treasure. I take a cat to my breastless panting. I leave the windowpanes all in wrenching tact, and step carefully over a coiled cable.

I'm telling you what I was doing out there alone at night meeting that sort of—in an unlit, desolate—

In the brain there's a mutilating wire that runs from hilt to shame in the name of memory. Barbed fatty brain, whose spikes make slut-raid on every whorled thing there, a stump. A puzzler. Screwed in gob-tight as a bulb, pulpy lamb flash gasping through its lacerated cask. Its hood. Or caul. Lodged there with baby spring's fuckfrost retributions that garbled, gray, speculative loser. It's a party. Impromptu. Guess what weeps out, now? Love? You know where we're headed? Any floor can be the killing floor—

Which is how we can remember the peopled world, filled as it is with plastic constraints. A line of rock salt between my fearsome and yourn.

I like girls, but I like boys better. For awhile, we only have two choices.
I like boys to hurt me, so it sounds like I don't like girls, it sounds like I
don't like anything but the part where boys get on top of me and my ribs
begin to crack. I like the part where the sick green fumes make a bag for
my head. I'll do anything dirty as long as it's clean. I scour my boyfriend's
cock. I dip his cock in vinegar and hold it under for two minutes. It
comes up gasping, clean as the future, it goes anywhere.

I hold hands with girls and braid their hair and follow them around
humming radio songs and change all the pronouns. I find a girl who has
the house all to herself and I get her down in the basement. I find a girl
to watch dirty movies with and then afterward we scramble. I find a girl
whose mouth I can practice on and whose body I can practice and I try
on all her clothes and find a pair of cut-off shorts that I wear for a week
without panties, but then my boyfriend comes over and I'm cocked up
with stupid all over again.

At the party someone has for graduation or for getting home from rehab
or because someone else's parents dropped dead and now someone
has a lot of money, I go into the home office with one of the girls and
we take turns sitting in the desk chair with our tits out spinning each
other in circles until the boys come in and start placing bets. After that
I refuse to put my shirt or bra back on and refuse to get in the car with
my boyfriend. A couple of the boys try to lick me and tell me my tits
make me look very young, they call me sweetpuppycockerspaniel, so I
get a beer from the cooler and drink it standing in the driveway all alone
while the sun comes up—

I might as well ask you. Why does everyone come to my window and then ask me to put on a robe or just fuck off? Why does everyone start a band halfway through the hand job and run out to practice? And why does everyone have some kind of car they want to tumble into head first slightly concussed and laughing throatily all the way to the ravine? Why do all the boys I love climb up on the trestle that runs over the ravine and slink down to its rusting-out catwalks and hold on infantile, lemur-like with all four limbs while the trains, only freight trains, rumble over?

Why, in the ravine, do I never find anything shinier than a beer can and never get anyone out before the cops come? I think I can die and then there we are up against a train and I think, oh, it isn't that easy after all. But I might as well ask you. Coded all these years as a boydigger, coded as a kissless dogface. They get so disappointed by my mustache. They get so angry when I make a joke, I'm changing the subject, I am changing the object from comely to homely from cumzy to hidden. They ask me if they can dig out all my blackheads. They have a hundred rules about how boring I am. I stay up the latest, you know. Out of all of them and all of you, I'm the last one with her lid laid open, a boiling beetsugar stew predawn premonition boiling over, a nosebleed. Or actually it's just common sense. You're going to jail and all of these boys are going to jail and all of these girls are jailed and all of these trains are going to jail, and if the trains even have conductors any longer also jail, and the rest of the town is basically jail and if you get into bed you get into jail and then there's the morning it's a penitentiary for you and yours—

Your Ugly Little,
Scab

Dear Mom and Dad,

Though I'm horrified by the sheer number of animal pounds you consume in a year, I find myself mouthing a fistful of ham. I find myself baking the dead into any available grain, into any tumbling sugar shack catastrophe. I do laundry. I shove a box of dead into the washer and listen to their skulls clank against the barrel. I vacuum their hair from my skirt, and can't figure out why I'm wearing the skirt's ugly announcement. I neither sweat nor dampen any longer. In the evening, the table will be piled high with steaks and lamb tongues whose campy bleat can't be drowned out.

I'll never understand what this red liquid is. It isn't blood, is it?

Consider the trade. We take two shotguns into the city. We take a box of ammunition and we wear sunglasses. It's August, and Dad has his suit coat buttoned. I've bleached my hair. We take the shotguns into the store swiftly. We hand them over and leave with a box of herbs and vitamins, which I proceed to swallow until ten years later the swollen lumps in my throat, chest, armpits, thighs, groin all but disappear. In that sense, when I leave you for dead I'll feel a pang of guilt.

It's the bleaching hour. I take your wedding album out on the back porch, mid-January and my breath comes an ice huff. My skin sticks to the clasp and tears away, fingertips going white on the fake white leather fake gold scroll, and only the bleach stays liquid, coat after coat. I'm also going to bleach you in your sleep. I'm going to put a funnel between your pillows and bleach you from the underside. I'm going to feel so cheerfully possible, it's always like this, every time science makes a promise. I go reeling out into the cold with my little prayer face all tipped up and shining, I believe things. I'm sure I'll get a nosebleed that tells the future, I'm sure I'll get a sign, my hands whispered tight like snake babies and my faith giggling up a fat bubble of woozy *please*. Or maybe that's just begging. Anyhow, I buy my own bleach, and mix up a paste that I apply to all the framed photos and all the certificates of merit. I bleach the contents of the deli drawer in the refrigerator and bleach out the inside of the Canadian V.O. bottles. I bleach the deer's head perched atop its own folded hide, and while I'm in the freezer, I bleach the ice. I bleach my breath so it'll never smell anything other than absent, I bleach each of my tears in a special saucer I keep for bleach and tears, and then pour them into an atomizer, but I never actually use this on you or the boys or myself or any of my ugly old teachers who are just begging for it.

I write a letter in bleach and then bleach it because of all the times I said *I'll die if you don't* and all the times I used the word *beautiful* to describe what's really just a scrawny stench of a boy. I bleach his address and his phone number, which is still on my inner arm and my inner thigh in permanent marker, and on my neck and the arch of my foot, part of it on my labia, I take a bleach bath, I bleach my towels when the numbers rub off and then I bleach my bleach until I've got the clearest glass of nothing you've ever seen.

I kind of like how much you hate me. I kind of like the way you push my face in my dinner plate and tell the waitress not to bother.

I can't go to sleep until I do something really special. I've got six pounds of sugar and a blowtorch, I've got burns on my hands already and burned sheets, but I'm not as good at it as the other girls. The girls my boyfriend writes songs about, the girl who lives across the street from him with her curtains open and live flames licking out the window.

How she ever managed to make such a mess, how she imagined herself in the movie and wore the clothes from the movie and reenacted the part of the movie where all the girls get cut up with their own knives or whatever stick and glass are lying handily around. How she ever managed to get her own mother to tear out such a hunk of her hair and stuff the hair down the garbage disposal until it protested and spat all the night's dinner back. How she ever managed in tap pants and heels to make it as far as the mall. Like every other kind of girl she puts her lipstick on in the reflection of a chrome bumper and rips her collar and takes a punch like a pro and goes with a trickle of blood so becoming and a bruise under her eye like a secret letter under her lover's pillow, every night a camellia blooming below her waterline.

What am I, yellowing thing with a skinny lip perched on a fat lip popping open to let anyone in or out? So I can't go to sleep. I let the yowling cat in the screen and out the screen I spill some puke, and then I start again with the sugar and this time matches and a set of tongs and a spiked heel I dug out of the trash in the dead neighbor's yard, the heaving among the willow trees with forty years of uncontestable dissatisfaction.

I took a frame, I took the preserved paw of her nasty dog that used to nip our cheeks and behinds, I took a repulsively pilled heating pad and an unopened package of doll needles. I took a package of crackers, opened, and one cellophane sleeve untouched, I took a lipstick labeled envelope with a series of X-rays of two different skulls.

I took a child-sized spoon and fork, a copy of our local telephone book from twelve years before I was born, I took her personal address book, one of many from a brown paper sack in which there were address books and rubber gloves. I took a can of hairspray and a bamboo trivet, ace bandages stained with iodine, a tackle box full of safety pins and lawyer's bills, clippings about prostitution rings and Catholic priests in scandal.

I found an uncured raccoon skin cap and vomited as quietly as I could into a pink plastic tub. I loaded my treasures into plastic bags and heaved them, then myself, over the fence so that her daughters wouldn't see, or train their red eyes on my back, or come to my door and ask me if their mother loved them, because I don't know. I don't ever want to speak to another daughter in the moment she considers the caramelized mound of shopping lists and receipts for medication, the hairnet, the plastic salt shakers, the yellow knee-highs and the pale violet ribbon glued cheaply to a snap barrette.

When I consider the time by turning around an alarm clock with luminescent dial and crabbed tick, when I consider the medical tubing and the silicone pump. I cannot go there too deeply, knowing that a daughter is herself an act, a minor devastation that occurs in dark suburban closets like—

Your Ugly Little,
Scab

Dear Mom and Dad,

I'm puking my guts out from meeting all these twins of mine. Everyone has been told how boring her prose is or has peed herself in public again or has become the dull and vast girl-shaped graveyard. Here comes my twin with the scar in her navel, her box of bitters and her paint thinner visions. Here comes my twin with his boxcar compromised, very upset about the new administration. Sometimes when I'm wracking back and forth on top of a body I can hardly stay put.

Here go my mechanical limbs in a doll-shaped drive.

All my rights are alienable. That I hold onto them for the time being is material. I might pull my breast out and shriek when it's offended. I might not pull my breast out. My breast is small, targeted, fetid, prudish, hot to the touch, infected, swarming, bedecked, pierced through, has sleep in the eye, makes it clear that I am on borrowed time. All my privileges are plenty suckled up around me at night in the bed when I dream of getting out of here, of getting a pretty boyfriend who loves my face, when I dream of getting in good with all the girlbangfutures and forming a party, and I dream of the dress I will wear to the emancipation of all bad feelings. I pray to be a beautiful actress and model whom everyone loves and also for all the cats to be relieved of their despair and the dog never to suffer loneliness and also for all the strangers whose diseases and failures I'm unable to catalogue. My prayer is addressed to the heart of the construction, to the gear from which all shafts emanate. I am a white girl in a headdress. Costume is a privilege. As are ostrich feathers as are gestures made with the ringed hand as are tilts of the head. My privilege gets sawn in half two-for-a-quarter and I gape in mirrors at my own torso mounted on a butcher-block trolley. Time and a half.

Everything I shave off grows back in a matter of days, everything I bleach resurfaces, there's nothing I can do but proliferate. I've been bleeding since the Gulf War, even though I can hardly keep my eyes on the news, and I'm not part of the community of people like you who keep voting for the right person all knowing ahead of time who will be popular. I keep choosing Mondale. I keep choosing a woman or a terrier or a snowflake for office. It's twenty-five degrees below zero and I go out in a t-shirt to see how fast my sweat will freeze. I go out with a boy upstairs in my bed writing a letter to the editor about how much he loves the old men who give him pot and literature and how much he hates the old men who take his pot and literature away. He's writing a letter to the editor about what a spoiled princess I am, about how I have three twenty-dollar bills in my underwear drawer, which is true, I got them for doing a job and I keep them for an emergency, but by the time I get back, they're in his pocket.

I say nothing. I feed him a butterscotch. Truthfully, I don't even notice. I'm such a privileged whoresack, I don't even think about money. I wear a Marxcuff as punishment, around my neck. Its fluted ruff gags me, and I vomit down my front.

I feel my cells dividing. I feel my cells manufacturing fat from food and manufacturing other things like keratin and hormones. After the boy leaves with my money and my copy of *Dharma Bums*, I turn off all the lights and eat one hundred raisins. I eat one hundred bites from an apple, I eat one hundred cereal flakes. I take one hundred sips of water, I floss my teeth one hundred times, I pick one hundred flakes of paint off the window frame, I make one hundred check marks in my diary, I take one hundred shallow breaths in quick succession. I sit cross-legged exiling thought until my legs aren't only weeping from, but become one hundred brutal axes, and sit longer until I can forgive each axe its brutality and longer until the axes move as tools in a natural order without motivation, until never again is it a hand that wields a tool, welds itself to a tool in confident assumption of the role but that these things just are, after all, hacking metronomically into the uncooperative citizen until her meat suit is its own stocks.

Outside, the temperature stalls so far below zero it appears to be dead. Outside the temperature counts the bodies. Absolutely no one goes to war. Absolutely no one calls it by name–

Taped to the underside of my underwear drawer. It's a fickle sliver
beating up our chests, isn't it? Every day is numbered, and then the
numbers repeat until you take out your contraband pistols and wave
them at the roots. I'm calling up into the crawl space, got room inside?
Got room inside for me to crawl–

After three months of not eating, I have fifteen crackers and swell
right back up to prosperity, adder-puffed, clumsy with flesh, rich as a
pharaoh, rich as butter, a lump of butter, unmeltable, not on a tongue,
not in a fire, cold, damp, thick as the future, a brick, a ton, a captured
stuttering liquid, the slowest beat available.

With a handful of myself and handful of my hair, I'm tugging through the
door. I'm tugging out into the night, a fractured whirl, a stumble. In
my sock paws, digging through the yard to its furthest edge where it hits
road, where ants and worms come into contact with the inexplicable,
with that for which they're not genetically prepared. Where everyone's
altered. In the squealing advance of boys, I pull myself together and
shove it all into a stiff leather coat. I'm covered in carcinogenic dead.
I'm inhaling its treatment, my warpath. My hair begins to fall out and I
facefirst across laps, I'm secured with a furry forearm, with a bottle of
Wild Turkey, I giggle it down.

In the future, when I'm bleeding out all over my bed any hope I ever
had of passing, I'll remember the smell of whiskey that needs a cleaning
and upholstery that needs a cleaning, cracked plastic edges, copper
hot thighs in ripped denim, little hairs bristling through the ultra-soft
lattice, chives skunk over-ripened breath. No dogs, no bikes, no books.
Nowhere to sit that isn't going to stain. Nowhere to rest my head. No
window that isn't smeared thick and ashed out. No songs on the radio,
no jokes that make nice, no whisper of encouragement. Flashlights, no
food. Broken strings, broken bits of plastic, empty soda bottles, maps of
towns further north. Territory.

Shoved up against the rear windshield, a carton of cigarettes, a stiff
greasy towel. In the future, when I've slid greased out of this past, I won't
forget what it smells like. I'll hate the summer for it, I'll wish I gave a yell,
I'll wish I hung my head out the window and begged them to go faster,

I'll wish I had more than a dollar on me when we stopped for meds, I'll wish that I'd known my blood was a renewable resource.

I see water on the road. That's what I repeat. Water in a panic, a panic lake of water coming up between the overpasses and off-ramps into the fleshy machine light of a city well past its boom. I hear it splashing up over the tires even as the vision clears and the boys howl and pinch me in the sugar-soft strung out rib flesh. I cock my head, a pet, and everything goes dry.

I'm just like a kitten, like a ballerina kitten, like a kitten ballerina swan queen, like a princess, like one of you, like my breath stinks, like I went to bed with a baba full of bourbon milk and Xanax, like I look like you no matter how many times I scratch up my face, like I got your face on my face. Like I'm going to be as fat as you someday. As white as you, I'm never going to get out of this sleek white luxury sedan with the trunk full of bodies and hoaxes. Like I'm never ever ever ever going to get drunk again. Get laid. Get my legs open on the back seat of this car, it's idling, it's sprawled in the yard, there's a blue tarp leaking off it into the yard. The yard's frozen. There's trash of the worst kind, things that were once in the body, things that were once under the hood. Even though you're so fucking rich. I saw a kitten a couple yards away. I'll never have a kitten again. I won't hold something soft and half-formed as a kitten. Or touch it. I tape up my hands before bed. I don't actually sleep, but I get in the bed and I lie perfectly still like an ape in ice.

My paws scarcely articulate. All my jittery digis, nail beds scavenged, whiten. For a solid month I've been performing like a good dray, up at dawn, and sketch sketch sketchy my height on the wall. A good breakfast of yum-yum, a good dose of down-down. Clean paws clean maw clean panties for good measure. In the morning, jobs wait, raking, stacking, sanitizing. For some reason, we can't let even the flattest possum stay singed to the pavement. On a stick, we carry a stench not normally found in the human world.

Here are my crafts, all manner of flora glued to the floorboards, all sorts of wire stacked neatly by beads, nothing puncturing, nothing decomposed. Here are my records of what I've eaten and when I've come and gone. Here is the lock on my bedroom window, intact. But I'm bored. I'm swishing my tail this way and that in contemplation. I'm stalking a good time in my head. What's there to do around here but eat snacks and weep? I empty your drawers and take whatever pills I find. I smear blood and make-up on the good towels, I press one of the onyx pawns from the chess set deep into my filigree, I disassemble the microwave and then strap it back together with rough twine and paper clips. I stitch every glove and mitten I can find onto my pants, and flap my way into the yard, the sweetest angel farmer, the yardbird from a fairytale. I coo.

Neighbor, neighbor, I coo. Neighbor, neighbor, come get a little corn, a little strip of potato skin. Come closer, little nuzzler, bring your snout up my thigh, give a little gust of hot breath, give me a sign, beast, scratch my name in the dirt.

Oh, neighbor, there you go again, roughshod over my face. There go my stitches, pop pop. There you go tearing back across the street, street-wise, dry as a fig. Why do we live here? None of our neighbors can give me a good scare, none the dickens, none the lost-luggage shame tag. No one holds a match to the side of my face, my head turned sharply, while he pushes me up against his living room wall. No one hisses in my ear while we watch business as usual out the window, mail delivered, children peddling, no one says it, I'm hardly worth the effort, but he'll kill me to shut me up if he has to, now that I know, and hands me a shovel and tells me to wait for dark.

That's it. We live on the boringest street in town. I stretch out on the pavement, where nothing rolls in but stray cats. The neighbors hate us, with our overturned lid from the garbage can filled from two ten-pound bags of cat food, feeding weasels, raccoons, groundhogs. A fat lonely groundhog lives under our pool shed, wheezing from chlorine, addicted to Cheetos. In the shed, everything hums, and without the shed everything shrieks bright. Children, NutraSweet-riddled, pile onto an inflatable raft, shiver, succumb to horseflies in the deep end. Swim face up to a dead bat, swim face first into a colony of moths, a pollen sheath, slip out of the pool with a fine layer of Gramma's saliva settling over our skin, it's summer, a cold summer, refusing to start.

I'm aware that some boys want to touch me, and others want to touch someone else. It's a lazy easy thing to know the limited market value of one's own tweaked margin. I take it with me everywhere. The hotter it gets the more I can sell off, and there are the boys drowning in their own sweat, clear-as-a-bell sweat, sweating it out, waiting, and there I am with an ice cube clenched in my fist and an ice tongue and a freezer burn. A sorry refuge, but in the cool dusk, oh, don't be dull forgetful angry with me. Or, I find it so hard to stay angry with you for so long, like a job, like a fulltime occupation of—

My boyfriend promised to take me out into the woods where we'd live on biodiesel and shit at the base of trees. Where we'd stack up permaculture terraces and farm our own darkofnight mushrooms. Where we'd truffle like pigs and speak the original language. He says he doesn't believe anything you told him about my dumbbitchheart. He shoos the kittens out of the kitchen sink and gets me a glass of water. It's the nicest thing anyone's ever done for me. I won't drink it. I'll keep it forever, I tell him I'm going to keep it forever. He tells me that when we leave we can turn the gas on and the lights out and nail a two-by-four over the window.

But then he leaves town alone. He gets a job walking the perimeter of state parks and making out with lonely hikers. He gets a job selling truckers a compound of herbs and ethanol. His job is to keep his name out of the papers. His job is to put children back together with loose matches and a box of Steri-Strips. He leaves town without me. I find myself with a lot of time on my hands, so I learn to make incisions. Then I learn to make small doses of chlorine gas. I take a staple gun to all the curtains, I paint the names of show dogs in black nail polish on the living room carpet. I'm so lonely, I can't stop reading the books on alien abduction.

I try to past-life regress myself, and wake up with one of the kittens retching into my lap. I shave my legs, I shave off my pubic hair, I pluck all the hairs from around my nipples, I reduce my eyebrows to thin arcs of ghostwhite flesh. I volunteer at the only hospice where the dying don't feel the need to speak politely. I try to volunteer at a center for the developmentally challenged, but a boy I used to fuck works there and thinks I've come because I'm pregnant so tells the receptionist I'm stalking him. She walks me out to my car and gives me a package of Fig Newtons and a cigarette and tells me she'll have to call the cops and men are shitforbrains, anyhow, you know.

I work in a soup kitchen, I place calls for a telethon, I'm always hanging

around the neighbor whose brain was pierced by a metal pipe. I learn
sign language, I wear a dog tag that alerts medics to a seizure condition
I don't have, I learn to fake a seizure, I learn to take my tongue far back
in my throat and kill my bladder. I walk with a limp, I lose fifteen pounds,
I wear no make-up, everything I eat turns to stone. While eating a
chicken sandwich from the fast-food drive-thru, I hallucinate bells, I see
straight through the room into the past. I see the cult leader who loved
me before I was born, everything smells charred, I can feel the scorch of
an incense stick on my lower back. I take the test to see if I'm worth an
afterlife. Is it a pyramid, you ask me, is it a square, is it four wavy lines, is
it a sphere with an arrow? Is it?

Beside the kittens, the parakeets, and the fish, lie the dead dogs drowned in the hole in the house in the basement that's always filling with water. A cataract eye floats wearily up to the surface. A box of fat books seething musty, a box of ammunition, a box of small records, all blank. What am I doing here, scumming around in your scumbags?

If I could tie anyone up in the basement, in the garage, the little attic-like hutch beneath the dormer, and give him a blue plastic pail to piss into and give him a sandwich and pretend like I forgot his hands were tied and tie him extra tight because I'm prepared for this. I am *prepared* for this.

Like any house, we have mice, and they die of exposure. To the chemical. I write all my loveletters in chemical and set them on fire in a tin drum in the basement. I piss in the blue pail myself to test it out. I try the ropes against my wrist. I consider the rags. I'll have to wash his face, I'll have to keep him clean in ways no one else does. If I could have anyone, I'd bind him to a chair and wedge the chair between the wall and the furnace. He'd like his nest, lined with my t-shirts. I fill three plastic jugs with water, and collect a dozen old paperback books, grizzly romances and supernatural thrillers. When one of the kittens follows me, I scold, no no, it's for him. It's for that boy I'm getting. Why is he taking so long?

I pace the street looking for him. I rip the sleeves off a jean jacket and install speakers in the breast pockets. I play the same album at top volume over and over again. Your love is like bad medicine, bad medicine is what I need. I lie down in the street with my nearly invisible tits blasting. Ain't no doctor that can cure my disease. I'm girls, girls, girls. I'm teasing my hair, teasing my skin, teasing what remains of my muscle tissue. I've got my jeans on so tight I can travel back in time. I'm filleted with zippers. The lighter in my pocket catches my pocket on fire. I'm looking for a boy to come back by here, whose high-top sneakers hang loose as hooves. I'm looking for a boy whose dark hair drips greasesorrowfangvenom. I'm looking for the geometry of contraband in his back pocket and the evident crush of his balls. When he gets here we'll know it's him by his breath rank with hallucinogens and his second-rate terror seizure accusing *gonna eat me*.

Everything's ready. I flip through a magazine. I try not to disturb the old sleeping bag I've unzipped and spread over the chair, try not to leak on its mallard duck lining. I flip through a magazine. Thighless thighs, fractured ribs, netted face restraints. Lovers. I make myself a face restraint out of dental floss and rubber bands. I sit still. He's taking forever. I flip through a magazine. Tangled hair masks. Bird's nest cunt. Stretched canvas limb flag, fellatio nation.

I crouch in the woods with his arm lodged inside me. We're married and he uses my hair to scrub the bathroom floor. We're married and he uses my tongue to check the oil, he uses my eyelashes to strain the grease from the bacon pan, he uses my upturned pelvis to hold his bottle caps. He buys me a pair of stockings made out of lamb's wool and formaldehyde. He makes a plaster cast of each of my legs and of my crevice. He makes a plaster cast of my diary and then burns the diary in the charcoal grill. He carves his name in my fender and pushes the car slow and dreamily off the cliff. We catch a rat and split it between us. In the basement apartment, we find a mosquito queen and her cast of vagabond kittens. We're sitting wearily beside each other on a floral sofa waiting for our names to be called. *These are the lamps in the waiting room for Hell*, I say. *This is where pesticides come from*, I say. We have to get our faces lifted. He's gone through three gallons of water and I can't get home in time. We've gone to war and in the trench I roll him over and in each of his sockets I find a diamond, right before my own bomb goes off. I wake up panting, and dressed like a widow. I'm wearing one of his pubic hairs in a vial around my neck, which even I know is in poor taste, I'm not so stupid as all that, but oh am I lonely–

Your Ugly Little,
Scab

Atrocities in April

Bay of Pigs, Beirut U.S. Embassy bombing, Black Hawk, Black Sunday storms, Boston Marathon bombing, Chernobyl disaster, Chicago April Fool joke Frank Linnament killing, Columbine, Donner party starts out, Fort Hood shootings, Germanwings crash, Great Mississippi flood, Highway 410 concrete barrier crushes family, Hillsborough disaster, Hitler born, Lincoln assassination, Ludlow massacre, Martin Luther King Jr. assassination, McDonald's opens, murdermurder, Nigerian schoolgirls kidnapped, Oklahoma City bombing, Pierre Curie run over, raperape, San Francisco earthquake, SS Sultana explosion, Scottsboro Boys sentenced to death, South Korean Sewol ferry tragedy, Revolutionary War British invasion, Texas City explosion, Tbilisi tragedy, Titanic, USAAF Mortsel Belgium bombing, USS Iowa explosion, Unabomber final bombing, Virginia Tech shooting, Waco siege, Walter Scott shot in back by police officer, West fertilizer plant explosion, Yom HaShoah, Yuma AZ twin toddlers drown–

Dear Mom and Dad,

No one wants to embarrass himself yakking up my name on the lawn.
No one really wants to get stuck watching me, marking time while I shed
my clothes. So I set myself up in the yard. I set myself under an overripe
mulberry tree, and the fruit leaks down my dress. Soon I'm sticking like a
blue-black fly on her back in the honey pot, a field of flies come to roost,
come to seethe, a mass of hungry mouths and impatient forelimbs. I'm
ready to be collected. I'm ready to be skinned and pinned, examined for
educational purposes, set aside in a drawer, sealed in a case of my own
refuse.

I spread myself out in the lily bed, stems wrecked beneath my stems
wrecked, the peony petals turn flesh in my breath, the blackberry
bushes bee-swollen, fogged up with pollen lust. Everything in the yard is
startlingly alive on the verge of decay. The pungent bloom of impatient
lifecycles, everything buzzing until I can't bear it and I rush to get your
rusty clippers from the bucket in the garage, but instead of trimming, I
come up short a warped leather trunk, a skin coffin for the past, a living
dead hope chest, an animal choked full of your indiscretion. Dead moths,
a set of wrinkled sheets stained with their decade of origin, the scuzzy
smell of burrowing. In here, a tape recorder plays hideous old-time
matinee losscore, its blue button glistens candy gag.

On a thread wrapped round your eyetooth and slid down into your gullet
you can hang any secret you like, cough it up at leisure. Can't you. I dig
through the trunk looking for my real name, a birth certificate, a warrant.
I swallow a matchbox, some plastic beads stained around their seams,
kitten eggs, a bottle of early generation mood stabilizers. I take a nap on
the grease-stained concrete. When I die, my grave will be heart-shaped
and pulsing.

Don't you love my hair in hanks? Don't you love me coming to, fumbling the backs of my hands against my face? Don't you love my skin blurring off my face, awash in beetle shells and gasoline? And then I wait for the boy. For this or that spell-pants boy who will meet me in the garage. Who'll rub his flat hand against me and count to ten and shoot and go.

It's getting harder to tell them apart, each smelling like gas station snacks and pot smoke, the crap music they hack up on their guitars, each sucking a sweet sucker like a small child at night. I make each of them consistently uncomfortable. After sex I speak in a way that makes them feel they've fucked a relative. That makes them aware of all the wet spots and creates an impermeable loser zone. I'm always putting my mitts down an exhausted pair of pants, bored out of mind, time, money.

Oh, you guys know what I mean. How hopeless a life's work.

I try to leave, but I only make it as far as the gutter. That's a joke, guys. I try to leave and I make it far enough to buy a new set of tattoo needles, by which I mean safety pins. I call a girlfriend and she promises to do me later if I bring all the supplies. I find a bottle of vodka with the seal still intact and six ballpoint pens out of which I pop the ink tubes. I get a couple of pain pills from a guy at the ice cream shack, who trades them to me for one of my red painted nails clipped to the quick. Here on my gut it's going to say *never*. To say *I came here to do right, but I did wrong again. Leaky* or *flabby* or *ugly smells*. Nothing. A bent over stick figure puking into a bucket, that figure wearing the bucket over its head. The name of them whose life I ruined in blacked-out heartscript. In an eel heart, inside out, in a nest of treasure. In a nest of rotten teeth, pirate's teeth, why the hell not, I'm not shy. I tried to get away, but here I am strolling the shame arcades with a sack of dead daisies. Here I am upside-down on the tilt-a-whirl, yelling the lyrics to "Surrender." Here here here they come, some paramedics with their arms full of beer and blankets and ready to have a barbeque with me in the sandiest lot or dead-endedest alley, ready to make out inside a dumpster plastered with pictures of runaways. I can't get out of here. Not without some money.

Anyhow, she tattoos a misshapen skull, big, from ankle to calf, one socket x'd-out and the other one crying for its mama. I'm so grateful I myself can't stop sobbing, and she gets worried about her parents, so she stuffs a t-shirt in my mouth and then I'm the happiest I've been in months. I put my arms around her. I put my arms around her shoulders, which are narrower than mine, and I feel like I'm wearing a big pair of boots, kicking the fuck out of her row of china horses. I'm smearing blood and ink all over her white sheets and she can't stop laughing. We're going to be a little bit famous, we imagine. We're going to get out of here so late in the game, we'll be covered in welts and filled with the kind of neveragain you only see in the movies.

Your Ugly Little,
Scab

Know This,

In the future when I can't come to terms with my object status, when I can't stop the past from cunting up on me, when I become the pain artist whose limbs hurt, when I go forward with a chest full of cherry-picked daggers, lace, laced in, when the digital fails to reproduce the analog and so fails gender, fails heartthrobbing, when television rains down and washes us starry and clear, when the face of television can be scanned over all our scars, when it is my job to shuttle forth comfort, when I conduct myself like an adult across the asbestos plateau–

Then, fuckers, I'll get it wrong again. Don't think this is all barreling toward redemption. Don't imagine for one second the girl will purify our culture for us or that the illiterate moment will yield. In trenches, you lose it all over again. Never edifying, ever yours–

Your Ugly Little,
Scab

Dear Mom and Dad,

A bomb goes off. A shooter goes rampant on the other side of the island. In the living room, a bomb goes off, a star becomes a bomb, in the night sky a bomb is born. Tick tick, say the kittens. Tick tick. By the river, a bomb goes off. The school crumbles around its own dead star. The bee bomb goes off, tick tick, the bees. The phone rings a bomb in our sudden midst. The bomb rings and it's the sister of the dead girl, it's the friend of the sister, it's the police, it's the man who sold her all those hollowed-out books. The phone rings and it's the phone ringing out its own plastique ambivalence.

I've got a quart of gasoline and anxiety lodged in my chest.

Dear Mom and Dad, dear Mom and Dad, I'm out on the lawn yelling. The phone rings and it's me soundbombing you.

On the other side of this squalid series of hills, a bomb goes off. A car bomb goes off, a culvert opens, everything that terrifies the readers goes off, showering the news feed with debris. I mean, the memory gets reanimated in the future when electricity is our most subtle bitch.

I did wrong, Mom and Dad. I left my baby out unloved in the downpour, her little face in spasm, her little glum grief song wrecking the bandwidth. I did wrong, made as I am out of your spare parts, flunked as I am in your blood.

Dear Mom and Dad in the future when they make me a pill out of my own hair that's meant to raise the dead and inhibit the present tense, that's meant to reestablish the borders around my gut, that's meant to save my baby from a lifetime of get the fuck away from me, I'll take it and you won't recognize me, that's how bright I'll pulse in the measure before the bomb goes off, that split-second in which we live every tender morsel of stupid decay.

Dear Mom. And Dad.

Dear Mom and Dad,

Because I'm so undisciplined, there's a good chance someone will catch me writing these letters. There's a good chance someone will see me holding a wad of toilet paper against my crotch with one hand while with the other presses out the last of the pee. What is it you wanted me to do today? Eat this bag of red meat you left in the sink? Call the government and explain exactly why I've been using all that electricity? You wanted me to lie down in the airport looking pale until someone gave you a ticket to the clinic?

All I love is the melody and the cakes. Here is the trigger I'm reluctant to pull, and here is the dope I'm reluctant to smoke. Here is the completely full bottle of Jägermeister and here is the can of tomato juice I was going to pour into my shorts because really I can manufacture my own blood now and I won't do that in public. Anymore, I swear. Here is the dress I wear when I want to have sex in public, and here are the shorts I wear when I want to have sex in a crowd. Here is my receipt for latex. Here is my little honeysuckle, my sweet frenchie lush. I don't want you to think I'm dishonest, too. I'm compulsively honest, remember? Or else wouldn't I have a purse full of booted lip gloss? Wouldn't I have every cop in the gallery? Wouldn't my boyfriend stop calling me cheatingwhorebitch? And bring me along in his van?

I'm too honest to shower, and too honest to lie about cramming a stranger down my throat. I turn my panties inside out. I empty my pockets full of chewed gum and keys to the gas station's bathroom. Fat purple sow kisses ring my neck, so now I'm stuck home with a mouthful of loser cream, hanging out in the backyard where I try to bury my boyfriend's records, and then in the front yard where I try to burn his name in the lawn with gasoline, but everything's so wet from my sobbing, my spilling. My blisters burst on the good sofa and you send me to my room. There in my room

I lick the photogenic chemicals off every snapshot of us and I snip
his driver's license into a hundred pieces and I claw his name into my
dresser and I have a migraine that lasts for one thousand years and loves
me so much it may have to kill me. I change my last name, and wear
something it can sink its teeth into. Skin, eyes, sinuses. I'm exceedingly
beautiful in the light of the bare bulb hanging in the closet, gagging
through the door open a sliver, across the plastic shag carpet. I put my
head between two speakers and set the dial to scour. I've blown back
across the evening, blown back across intelligence, and here trickling
the remnants into a small paper cup all waxy under the fingernails—

In the summer camp for pythons, bad girls, and history buffs, I meet a CIA applicant. He's precise, trim, his glasses so polished they set fire to anything he looks at. He's coming my way with a question about literature, he's coming my way with a book of chubby sonnets in his pocket. He's rubbing his hands together with my thigh in between. He doesn't care if anything dead fell out of my crotch, he doesn't care that I am a teenage bride and my back is covered in sebum boils and cigarette scars and one look at me will ruin his career not because I've got anything special but because he'll get an indelible stamp of bad judgment.

He tells me how smart I am and asks to smell the inside of my sleeping bag. After lights-out he comes scratching at the screen trilling a night bird song, dressed as a raccoon, carrying an Edison. He crouches under the porch and waits for my ankle to brain him. He stands in the showers fully clothed, fists stacked under his chin, weeping, and when the water comes on he goes still until the shower fills with girls and if I'm among them he hands me the soap. When a possum is injured, he sits at its spitting bedside until the park rangers come for it. He eats with a knife and fork balanced easily in his competent fingers. During the evening prayer he replaces *our salvation most high most wholly large most immediately correct deepest influence so help me your grace* with my name.

Some of the campers know how to become lawyers and some will stop cutting themselves as soon as they learn about yoga. Some campers go home for holidays and eat the fleece right out of their bed pillows, and some die on the bus. I'm there to lose weight or to recover from a fit of consciousness. I'm there to wait until the bassist who keeps leaving dead snakes in our mailbox gets bored. I'm there to keep my mouth shut about the hotel rooms you've shot and the windows you've shot out and the tax returns you haven't. I'm there to shut up about the children in every state down the eastern seaboard, and there to shut up about the toxic rental properties and sham garages. I'm there to wipe the smirking scars off my face and to smirk no more when you receive a public award and to stop puking in the tureen and to stop jabbing guests in the side with the tip of an antique harpoon, the harpoon's rope wrapped around my waist, my arms wed to it, its blackened brass leaving a faint tang in the air. When you insist upon my departure, when you pay for it, when you bag me up and tie me to the bus rails, when you pack a bag for me and it contains pre-stamped envelopes and a stack of Saltines, when you charge me for it, when you write *clean up time* on my forehead in marker, magic marker, stinking like grape overdrive, when you rent my room out to a cult leader, when you burn my novels, when you slit the particle board back of my dresser and remove from its dark interior, should I go missing, my list of things you might've done to me, and burn it on the gas grill, and hand me a raw steak, and tell me I'll be leaving in the morning.

No one cares if the campers get high or have sex, so I do both and then go to the crafts tent to make myself another lanyard. At the end of the week, I've woven two sets of handcuffs and a ball gag out of bright plastic threads. With cotton loops, I've knotted together a horse suit. My hair hangs down, my mane down my back, my homemade hooves appear arthritic in the bad light of a burnt-out basketball court. There I do a dance I call *A Successful Morning of Vomiting Out All My Memories of You*. At the end, when I'm sticky from effort and my looped tail has gotten tangled in my bit, I scrub into the asphalt. The audience pokes me with the sharpened ends of marshmallow sticks while I make a noise I consider to be an abject whinny until one of the counselors clears a path and elbows me back to my bunk. There's a line of boys waiting to peek up under my horsey skirt and find out if it's true, but I'm so tired I just roll over and let them have at it–

This is ground zero for those with unusual enfacement. This is their tent city in which I'm sometimes welcome. A lending library features everything, which includes the television's anthemic bleating, the sadcore harp, Why are you smirking up your face making obnoxious facial scenes, touchscreens, microground coffee, antique rose-colored garments and a biographical history of the color pink, Sally Hemings, a spaceship, portable defibrillators, cat memes, nail polish that hardens to a ceramic finish, an ashtray repurposed from a railcar, inside-out pocket watches, strips of plastic with fine grit overlay meant to prevent slippage, a diving suit, the chain latch for a front door, size 7.5 bamboo knitting needles, a power strip, a dripping paper sack, avian themed silver pins, a polar bear's ear that appears much larger than one would expect without the context of the whole bear, a lock of hair from a seven-year-old white female, the braid of a ten-year-old Korean female, one strand from Kerala once belonging to an intersexed black fifteen-year-old, fingernail clippings, someone's mother, turmeric, fraying polyester dragon-patterned brocade-backed photo album export, metal-setting amp, dried four-leaf clover, dust, young adult historical novel about a pirate and a merchant's daughter, two Day of the Dead skeletons pushing an infant skeleton in a walnut shell pram, a #10 envelope with plastic address window, water-stained curtains, abalone, a faux brass fire poker, Erlenmeyer flask with crusted rim, diapers, sebum, orange plastic rabbit-shaped egg mold, lengths of black-gray and ivory tulle, a phenylephrine HCL tablet, Liam Neeson, hog bristle, nervous habit, castile soap, book binder's tape, staple gun, BPA-coated receipts, crumbling wings of dead Miller moths, barback's towel soaked in fulmaric acid, index pages from American Psycho, spice jar filled with soil from the volcano Hekla, linen notecards, underwire contour padded bra 36B in nude, a marrow spoon, irony, brake pads, 1/8 inch plastic pegs in pink blue red and white, an oak pew, thirty-pound bag of small stone white and light gray gravel, cold hands, striated throat, warbler feather, glass jar,

Your Ugly Little,
Scab

Dear Mom and Dad, the Past, Psssst, or Myself,

I miss him, I miss them. I don't miss you.

He won't talk to me on the telephone anymore. He won't let me get his
voice all chugged up inside my gaping holes like a substitute. When
people die, he hangs up on me. When everyone is dying he tells me
to call back later. He replaces his address with a latex glove. He never
knows me in the street.

One time we're sitting at the same table and it's our job to find out how
many scientists have been crammed end-to-end in the seafaring vessel
the poet made. It's our job to literally understand the cuddling that
takes place between one man of science and another who thinks the
mind is the brain and proclaims himself the god of science. I can't take
the intimacy. I take off one shirt after another until all I'm wearing is
a stained strip of cotton. *I've lost my pants*, I say, and regret it because
coming out of my mouth it sounds like the sort of thing an unshaven
man on the edge of the platform says, it sounds like pissing disoriented,
like a coin so thickly coated it no longer pings against the concrete.

When he won't talk to me any longer, I look for signs from him. He won't
appear in my dreams, so I'm left with sudden sharp pains in my gut and
anagrams in the obituaries. I'm left with counting the twists it takes to
break the stem of an apple or the thigh bone from the carcass or the
tooth from the mouth of the heavy bitchboy who keeps telling me how
incredibly boring I am like this is news.

I desperately want to tell him how much I will never talk to him again,
how none of his business it is who I've been fucking, how pathetic
his reliance on modernist thinkers, how unseemly his posture, how
unimposing his lip curled, how bland his t-shirts, how flat his jeans
flapping against his bone crotch, how tender, fuck it, how fucking tender
his voice when it splits from his best intentions, when it cracks against
his hard warm tongue stung with ash and cheap food, when he rubs
his salty hand against my morally inferior drudgecase, when we get

accidentally high at the same party and can't stop leaning up against each other because our hands are cranked and fused into those most basic haunts, because we love each other in a way that love means can't stop trying to clear the mud out of your airways. In the future when he comes to me full on corpse to register his disappointment in the wuh-wuh I've become, I won't hop the hegemonic vomit comet. I will tell him *ex-boyfriend-you never would've said this to me without binding my wrists.* I'll call him zombie and box his ears up. We didn't want to leave each other for dead, did we? We didn't want to use each other as the ladder out of town, but there wasn't anyone else whose bones stacked so well, whose tendons stretched so long, whose wicked face would dare you to. Are he the horsey I took to the border? Are he a whinny and I squirm in the saddle?

But all these pronouns are disagreeable. I only wanted to tell him that we're never doing this again. We're never again getting to the final scene and scrubbing me off. I walk out. I walk out on the wet grass at night and get my chest heaving like a scud. I go roaring forth into the beetle-backed night with no friends and no fear, every pitiful huffing breath cranking out of me like a hand job. Oh whatever, I loved you, I spent the whole cask, I spent every dime that would've been me, and I'd do it again to save us all from having to be ourselves in the future when we're way out of here and gagging quietly all night long, our only punishment for ever having been us, this ugly, ugly—

Here is a story: once upon a time a flab went walking in the wooded valley near her cottage. In the wooded valley, she came upon three pennies and a bear. The bear said, *these are my sister's eyes and her heart, help me return them to the sky.* The flab said nothing, for she didn't speak bear. *Give me your hand, flabby,* said the bear, and the flab said nothing, though she held out her hand, which was scarred from hot water and clenching a map. *Open your mouth, flabby,* said the bear, and the flab said nothing, but opened her mouth to receive the three pennies. The bear tossed her high onto his back, where she wrapped her scarf around his neck to make the reigns. The sun thudded into the wood and the bear leapt into the sky.

Every single constellation tells the story.

In the future, when I become the most earnest crepuscule in the heap.

You think someday that Dad will kill me, but it's Mom who'll do it. Slowly over a hundred years I'll die from all her will that's ailing.

Here are things that happened on the fairgrounds. A camel sat on a woman. A woman lost her ring and its finger when she climbed the fence after-hours and put her hand in the tiger's cage. The grandstand went up in flames. The water ran sour and everyone began to choke. In the middle of the night, children erupted in sores. In the middle of the day a man made of jerky sat under an umbrella with a shard of plastic in his teeth to make a bird's call. Where they sold a sack of needles and broken handles for a dollar. Where we sold a sack of needles. In my face the needle registered and it became clear that I was still in possession of my hymen, my hair, my quivering happenstance. I happened to be good at the ponies, I happened to weigh little enough that I could keep coming back long after the time had passed, and there I'd be, stale around the collar, filled with horseflies, pressing my face into a wad of spun sugar, and couldn't feel the rides.

It's language city. The cabal of nouns that does me in. They come toward me trailing their scents, a dead spaniel with his even more dead pheasant, whose wheels squeak, their slight flavor of metal on metal, metaphor loosing its linen. They stitch me into the hemispherical past. I'm not your girl, nor huffy King Henry's. Born in any other time, I'd have been just this raw mistake. The swan's wing crushing the fluted edge on the first attempt.

I'm joining the Holy Order of Cleanest Dead. I'm giving away every slutty stack of notebooks, every clump of hair from my brush. I get two bowls of bleach and soak my fingertips. It's time to clean you, too. I fill the microwave with your belongings and set it for forever. I develop a headache that clarifies my purpose in life: none. I pay the neighbor boy twenty dollars to tie my hands and feet together and prop me in a lawn chair. I wear a t-shirt that says PSYCHIC. I'm drooling a little from the pain, neat as a saint, trim as a martyr, pressed as primly between one page and the next as an accidental maggot. The moon inflates unbearably and I vomit, an empty hostage, a lidless tin the kittens lick until it rusts through to the sticky basement floor. Awash in caffeine and narcotics, my veins stinging and dilated, I wait for a car to pull in the drive. I wait for its headlights to wash me cleanest, for one sea to be supplanted by another, which scrubs harder than the first, for my shirt to get unstained, for my feet to touch sterile grass. Outside in the foul noise of small life, in the wet suburban smudge, medicine bride of medicine and plastic, stupid froth on my lips, vision fracturing until each streetlight's message settles legibly at my feet. The future comes to me as a series of car crashes and a system of grafts. The future is a dirty thing, breathing with its legs together just as fast as it can—

Your Ugly Little,
Scab

Dear Mom and Dad and a Lover,

I tell you all the time. *Heaven is a place on earth* where you tell me all the time *Heaven is a place on earth* where they tell you all the time this is your heaven. I tell you I'm coming home. When you get the news, you'll love me less than you ever did, and still, I'm coming home. When you get the news you'll never love me, I'll come home. I wanted to make something that put a quill through you. I wanted to make something barbed and oily, that took you hours to unsplinter, that took you to the ER with your blood in the lead, that took you the rest of your life coming back to. I got smart for you. I took all the books from the library. I stole books for you. From you. I stole your way of halting the room, your cross-legged way of walking, the pepper glass beads that make up your voice. Feet don't fail me, now. I'm walking home. I've crawled onto the back of a bear and mumbled *I'm a refugee.* Don't turn me down. Don't make me blue. I'm coming home. Where you have thickened. Where you have eaten every photograph so you won't have to remember. Where I won't have to remember. You're going to kill me when I get there. You're going to pull a hank of my hair so hard my heart stops. You're going to push my eyes deep back where they came from. You're going to grind my teeth into powder so I can't be called back. I'm coming home. Get out the rifle. I'm halfway there with my dirty jeans hitched lazily over my hips, with my boots full of emergency dollars. I'm coming home seventy-two hours straight through. I can't dial from here. I can't stand the sound of your voice over sixteen-thousand miles of satellite distance. I can't stand the sound of your voice in earbuds, right through my head a cyclone of disaffection. We'll get high. Don't make me sad. Again. We'll get through. I'm coming home to home to home to home to you.

Your Ugly Little,
Scab

Dear Mom and Dad,

In this adorable atrocity, every muscle comes alive—

It made me want to commit starry, starry death. It gave me a bullet wrapped in creosote, traveling at the rate of winter. It poured salt across my threshold, and over it I stepped. In a steel bowl, powdered chalk. In the future, when youaretheeverything cries out late at night, I'll do everything I can to brush it off. Lines of salt.

I wanted to make something clean. Don't you know? I wanted to make something that was not porous, no matter how closely you looked—and not you, but your machine, lens exponential in its uncompromising pronouncement. Something without fleck or pore, without texture. I wanted to make a surface that exceeded all classical efforts in its commitment to beauty. I did, then. Like everyone.

And everyone who waved a clean hand in this room, sitting at leisure with heads hung up by the song, with legs draped an emphasis on *leisurely*, with an ear to the wind stung mulberry whisper of some super-attenuated godvice. Everyone lying, and I with my ragged teeth was lying through them, too.

Did I lose my taste for beauty, or did I just cross into the room where its mask was worn? I don't have to describe to you the closeness of breath on latex. The concave interior, the skin-side of the cast, the wires in the dummy's noodle. Locked in the basement after everyone's gone for the day, when the pump starts churning, do I risk my pristine fine gauge thread? Do I come up nude from the inside out?

Whatever I did, Mom and Dad, I did in the loveless swan's gut of twilight. I did it on a lake with an oar through my heartlike organ. I did it skirts torn in the back field past sunset. I sat bare-bottomed on an anthill and begged for my life, for which the ants had no taste and I had no money.

Like everyone, I eventually pulled my hair tight up under a crown of lilies and proclaimed myself the good bride of keeping doors ajar. Between this realm of mouth speech and that other of minds pitching. I stood with my slippers pointing cold and beloved, one hand yawing into the cool clasp of the other.

In the future when my brute loyalty is safely torn out and pitched from

the window moving fast no plates, an unhinged notice will take its place.
I'll never again mistake the painter's eye for my own when reflected blue
and smug and full of anguish.

Your Ugly Little,
Scab

Acknowledgements

Excerpts from *The Book of Scab* appear as a chapbook CRAM in Essay Press's EP series #32, in *Black Clock*, *Everyday Genius*, *Fence*, *Interim*, PANK, *Women's Studies Quarterly*, *Wordgathering*, and *Yalobusha Review*. "All my rights are alienable" is derived from Roxane Gay's article on The Rumpus "The Alienable Rights of Women."

Bio

Danielle Pafunda is author of nine books of poetry and prose. Her work appears in a number of anthologies and journals including three editions of *Best American Poetry, Conjunctions, Fairy Tale Review, Kenyon Review,* and *TriQuarterly,* as well as the Academy of American Poets Poem-a-Day series. She has taught at the University of Wyoming, University of California San Diego, and University of Maine. She has served on the board of directors for VIDA: Women in Literary Arts, holds an MFA from New School University and a PhD from the University of Georgia, and can often be found in the Mojave Desert.